THE WHEELS ON

THE RACE CAR

BY **ALEXANDER ZANE** · ILLUSTRATED BY **JAMES WARHOLA**

SCHOLASTIC INC.
New York Toronto London Auckland Sydney
Mexico City New Delhi Hong Kong Buenos Aires

ISBN-13: 978-0-545-03028-1
ISBN-10: 0-545-03028-5

12 11 10 9 8 7 6 5 4 3 2 1   8 9 10 11 12 13/0

Printed in China

Book design by David Caplan

The text type was set in Coop Heavy.

The display type was handlettered by David Coulson.

RACERS . . . START YOUR

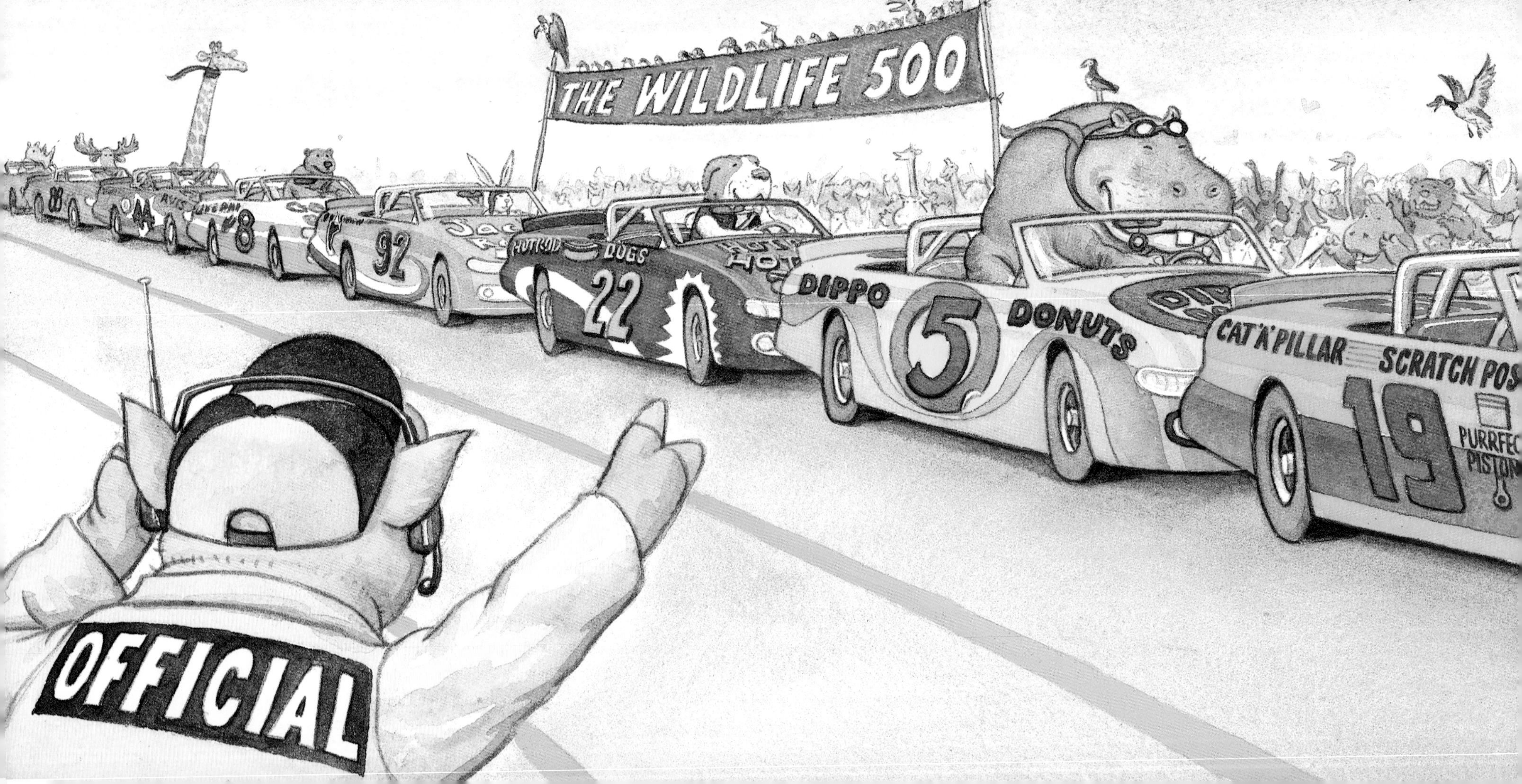

ENGINES!!!

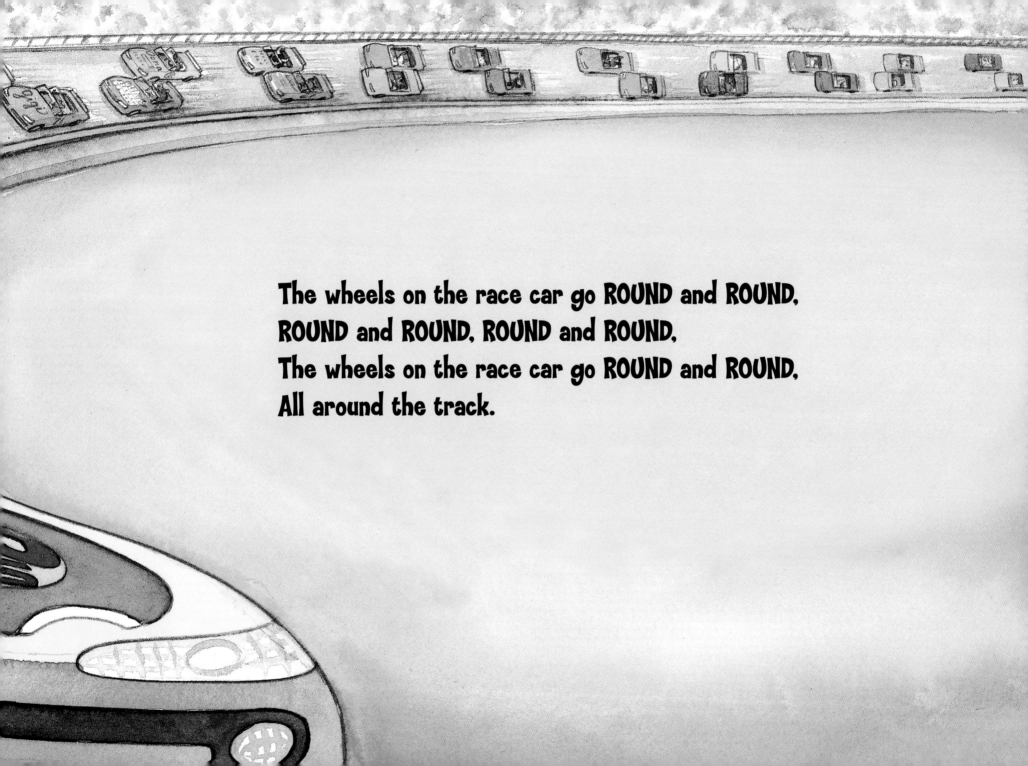

The wheels on the race car go ROUND and ROUND,
ROUND and ROUND, ROUND and ROUND,
The wheels on the race car go ROUND and ROUND,
All around the track.

The engine in the race car goes VROOM-VROOM-VROOM,
VROOM-VROOM-VROOM, VROOM-VROOM-VROOM,
The engine in the race car goes VROOM-VROOM-VROOM,
All around the track.

The driver in the race car yells, "GO-GO-GO!"
"GO-GO-GO!" "GO-GO-GO!"
The driver in the race car yells, "GO-GO-GO!"
All around the track.

The race car on the track goes ZiP-ZiP-ZiP,
ZiP-ZiP-ZiP, ZiP-ZiP-ZiP,
The race car on the track goes ZiP-ZiP-ZiP,
All around the track.

The driver in the race car STEERS and STEERS,
STEERS and STEERS, STEERS and STEERS,
The driver in the race car STEERS and STEERS,
All around the track.

The race car mechanics go ZIZZ-ZIZZ-ZIZZ,
ZIZZ-ZIZZ-ZIZZ, ZIZZ-ZIZZ-ZIZZ,
The race car mechanics go ZIZZ-ZIZZ-ZIZZ,
All around the track.

The gas from the gas can goes GLUG-GLUG-GLUG,
GLUG-GLUG-GLUG, GLUG-GLUG-GLUG,
The gas from the gas can goes GLUG-GLUG-GLUG,
All around the track.

The driver in the race car SPEEDS ON BACK,
SPEEDS ON BACK, SPEEDS ON BACK,
The driver in the race car SPEEDS ON BACK,
All around the track.

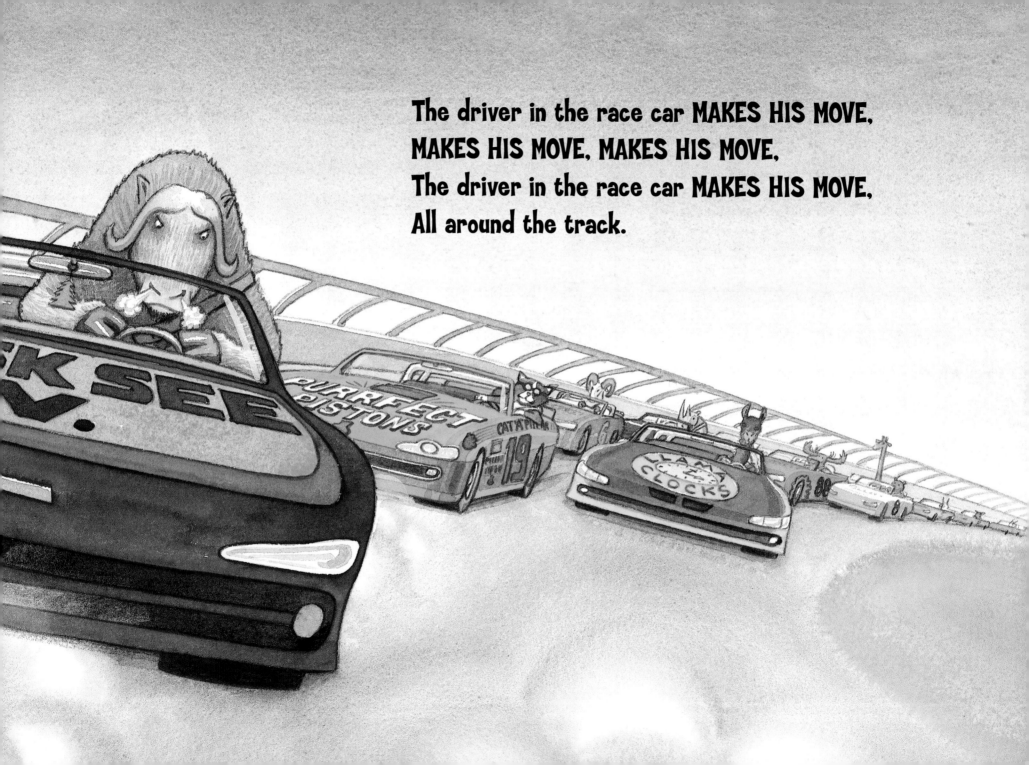

The driver in the race car MAKES HIS MOVE,
MAKES HIS MOVE, MAKES HIS MOVE,
The driver in the race car MAKES HIS MOVE,
All around the track.

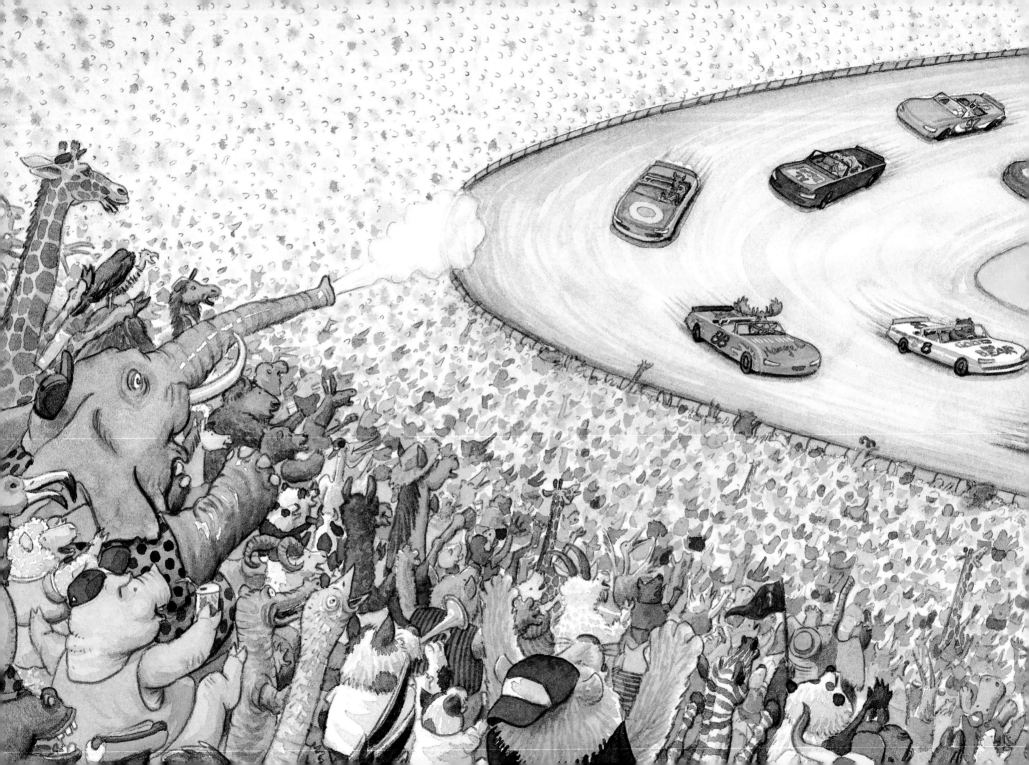

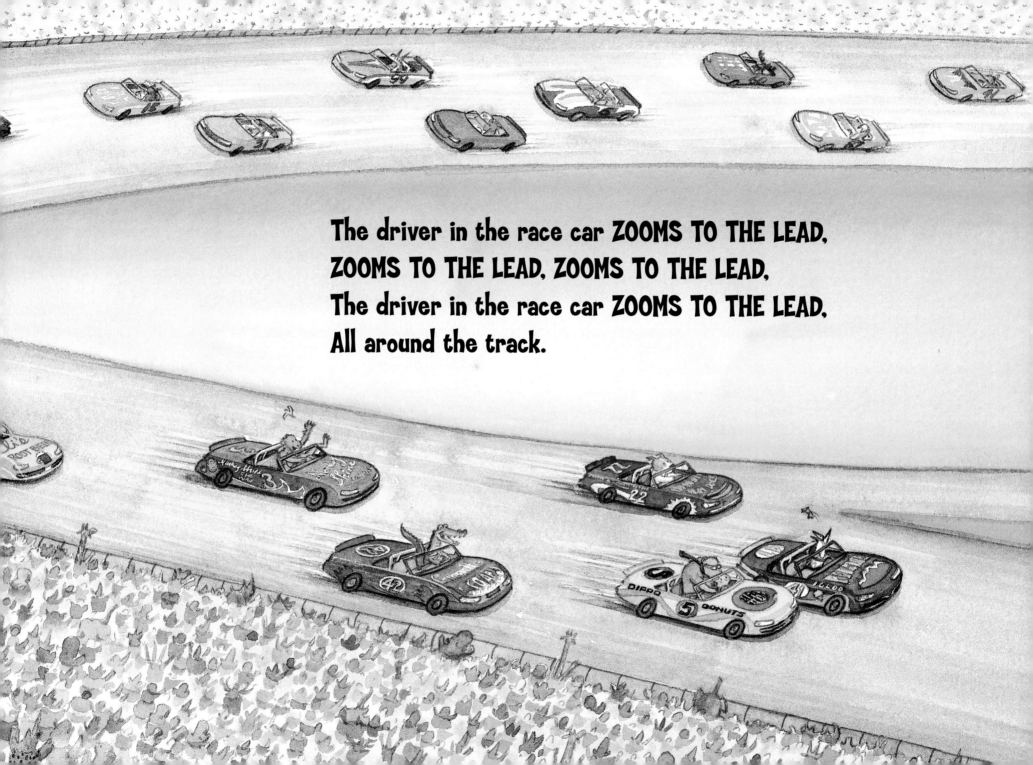

The driver in the race car ZOOMS TO THE LEAD,
ZOOMS TO THE LEAD, ZOOMS TO THE LEAD,
The driver in the race car ZOOMS TO THE LEAD,
All around the track.

The checkered flag goes SWISH-SWISH-SWISH,
SWISH-SWISH-SWISH, SWISH-SWISH-SWISH,
The checkered flag goes SWISH-SWISH-SWISH,
All around the track.

The wheels on the race car go ROUND and ROUND,
ROUND and ROUND, ROUND and ROUND,
The wheels on the race car go ROUND and ROUND,
All around the track.